Welcome to Paradise

Written by John Atkinson
Illustrated by Michael Engel

WINDWARD BOOKS INTERNATIONAL

Welcome to Paradise

ISBN: 0-929155-06-8

Published by Windward Books International
USA:P.O.Box 142, Lincoln, MA 01773
CANADA: P.O.Box 2329, Orillia, ON L3V-6V7

Welcome to Paradise

for all the
friends of the universe
everywhere

Chapter 1

"There it is," said Bamboo.

Everyone looked out the front window as they zoomed toward a planet which was mostly blue with large patches of white cloud cover.

"It looks just like home," said Josh.

"There are lots of places out here like your planet," said Windshield Wiper.

"With people just like us?" asked Josh's younger sister Mary.

"Let's just say there is life of all different kinds on most of them," said Bamboo.

Josh and Mary first met Bamboo and Windshield Wiper when they had came to help the animals at the local zoo. Mr. O'Greedee was the zoo-keeper and he was taking some of the animal's food money and keeping it for himself.

Now they were going to help some new friends. They flew on and were soon skimming over a huge body of water. There was no land in sight anywhere. In the distance a sun was just rising above the horizon and with it came the first light of day.

"It's an ocean," said Josh.

"This is just like home," said Mary.

"There are some things you will find a lot different," said Windshield Wiper.

"Like what?" asked Josh.

"You'll see," laughed Windshield Wiper.

Bamboo only smiled and steered across the surface of the water. A small island came into view and before long they were circling over the island and getting ready to land. The island was covered with ice and spread out across the entire surface were little black and white creatures.

"Those look like penguins," said Mary.

"They are," said Bamboo. "This island is the home of a huge family of penguins."

"Is that who we have come to help?" asked Josh.

"That's right," said Bamboo.

"What kind of problems could a bunch of penguins have?" asked Josh.

"We won't know until we get there," said Bamboo. "Now hang on. We're going to land."

As Bamboo gently set the ship down on the island, a few of the penguins gathered around to welcome the visitors. Josh was the first to get out.

"Hello," he said.

"Welcome to Paradise," said one of the penguins. "My name is Peter."

"You can talk?" asked Josh.

"Sure," said Peter. "Everything talks."

"Where we come from," said Josh, "the animals don't talk."

"Everything that lives can talk," said Peter. "You are just not listening."

The others got out of the ship and everyone talked and soon they were all friends.

"What a great place," said Mary.

"We thought you would like it," said Windshield Wiper.

"Come on," said one of the penguins. "Let's go for a swim!"

"Great idea! Let's go!" said some of the others.

All of the penguins standing nearby were the first to jump into the water.

"Come on in," they said. "The water's nice and warm."

Josh, Mary, Windshield Wiper and Bamboo decided to go for it and they jumped into the water with the penguins. Together they all played and splashed and laughed.

Soon a few of the local fish came over.

"Can we play too?" asked one of the friendly fish.

"Everyone can join in the fun," said Bamboo.

Then a dolphin came along and joined the party.

"My name is Captain," said the dolphin. "Anybody want a ride?"

Of course everyone wanted a ride on the back of the dolphin and so they all took turns holding on to the dolphin's fin and zipping back and forth across the water.

Josh was the first to notice a little fish which was trying very hard to keep up with all the others. It was a seahorse and although it swam as hard as it could, it never seemed to go quite fast enough and as a result, it was always being left behind.

"Hello there," said Josh to the little seahorse.

The seahorse smiled and said, "Hello. My name is Teacup."

"Nice to meet you," said Josh. "Are you having fun?"

"Oh yes," said Teacup. "I'm a little slow but I still like to play with all the others."

"Come on," said Josh. "Let's catch a ride with the dolphin."

"Let's go!" said Teacup.

And so the penguins and the fish and their new friends all played in the water. As Josh played with everyone, he wondered what problems Bamboo was so worried about. He would soon find out.

Chapter 2

Bamboo was the first to get out of the water. Everyone else soon followed.

"That was fun," said Josh

"Maybe we can all do it again sometime," said Mary.

"We'd like that," said some of the penguins.

"But first," said Bamboo, "we have some work to do."

"Can I help?" asked Peter the penguin.

"Maybe," said Bamboo. "We are here to talk to a penguin named Blue. Do you know her?"

"Everyone does," said Peter. "She lives with her group at the north end of the island. The rest of us live here at the south end of the island."

"You mean you have two separate groups of penguins living here?" asked Josh.

"That's right," said Peter. "Our leader's name is Pilot."

"Why don't you all live together?" asked Mary.

"No one knows for sure," said Peter. "That's just the way it is."

"Can you take us to see Blue?" asked Bamboo.

"No way," said Peter. "We never go up there."

The dolphin named Captain was floating nearby and she heard the whole conversation.

"I'll show you the way," said Captain.

"Thank you," said Bamboo.

"Can we swim that far?" asked Josh.

"Sure we can," said Captain. "I'll tow you."

"Let's go," said Windshield Wiper.

Bamboo, Josh, Windshield Wiper and Mary jumped back into the water and the dolphin towed them around to the north end of the island.

When they got there, they quickly found Blue. She and some of the north penguins were playing in the water. The slow seahorse named Teacup was also there to once again say hello to her new friends. After everyone had met Blue, Bamboo got right to the point.

"We have heard," said Bamboo, "that your island is no longer big enough for both groups of penguins."

"That's right," said Blue. "We are doing everything we can but the south penguins are just not co-operating."

"What do you mean?" asked Windshield Wiper.

"Over the years the number of families in our group has not grown much larger," said Blue. "And yet each year our island is getting more and more crowded. This can only mean that the south penguin families are getting much too big. And it's spoiling things for all of us."

"Why don't you just go and talk to them?" asked Josh.

"Never," said Blue.

"But why not?"

"Because it just isn't done," said Blue.

"But why?" asked Bamboo.

"Just because," said Blue.

This was all too confusing for Mary. As a matter of fact she thought it sounded kind of silly.

"We will have to go back and talk to the south penguins," said Bamboo.

"Yes," said Windshield Wiper. "We can talk to Pilot. Maybe he knows what is going on."

"I'll take you," said Captain.

"Let's go," said Windshield Wiper.

And off they went in search of Pilot, the leader of the south penguin group.

Chapter 3

Travelling all the way to the south end of the island took a little while. As they were being towed, Bamboo, Windshield Wiper, Josh and Mary pretended they were dolphins. They held onto Captain's big fin and rolled and splashed and had some good laughs. Some of the colorful fish followed along and pretended they were dolphins too.

When they got to the south end of the island the first penguin they saw was Peter.

"You're back," said Peter. "Did you find Blue?"

"We found her," said Windshield Wiper.

"And now we're looking for Pilot," said Josh.

"Is something wrong?" asked Peter.

"Yes," said Bamboo. "It seems your island is no longer big enough for everyone to live."

"It does seem to be getting more and more crowded," said Peter.

"Do you know where we can find Pilot?" asked Bamboo.

"He's not far from here," said Peter. "I'll take you to him."

They found Pilot playing with some of his friends and as soon as everyone had met each other, Bamboo got right to the point.

"Pilot," said Bamboo. "You must know your island is getting too crowded."

"Of course," said Pilot. "Everyone knows that. But we would not have a problem if only the north penguin families would stop growing so fast."

"That's funny," said Windshield Wiper. "Blue said the same thing about you."

Yes," said Bamboo. "She said your group was causing all the problems."

"That's not true," said Pilot. "Our families have not grown much at all. The only reason our island is getting crowded is because their families are getting too big. The north penguins are just not co-operating."

"Have you tried going to them and talking about this?" asked Windshield Wiper.

"We are waiting for them to come to us," said Pilot.

Mary thought Pilot sounded just as silly as Blue. Penguins are a funny bunch, thought Mary.

While everyone was talking, a group of fish gathered to listen in on what was being said. They all thought this was some kind of joke. But for the penguins this was no joke. Their island was getting too crowded and they were doing nothing about it.

During all of this, Josh suddenly noticed something strange. How can that be, thought Josh? He was going to say something to

Bamboo but then he decided there were more important things to think about and so he said nothing.

"Well," said Windshield Wiper, "I guess we better go back up to the north end of the island and talk to Blue again."

"Pilot," asked Bamboo, "will you please come with us?"

"No way," said Pilot. "I'm not going up there."

"Why not?" asked Bamboo.

"Because," said Pilot.

"Because why?" asked Bamboo.

"Just because," said Pilot.

How silly, thought Mary. How stupid, thought Josh.

Chapter 4

Captain was happy to take everyone back up to the north end of the island. Both Josh and Mary thought this was a great idea. They had a lot of fun being towed by the dolphin. But Bamboo had a better idea.

"Maybe we should walk across the island," he said.

"We can talk to some of the other penguins," said Windshield Wiper.

"I'll show you the way," said Peter.

"I'll meet you up there," said Captain.

"Let's go!" said Josh.

And off they went across the ice-covered island. Peter waddled along with his new friends. The island was quite crowded. There were penguins everywhere. They all said hello to the strangers who had come for a visit.

"Welcome to Paradise," they said.

"Where do you come from?" they asked.

Some were curious about the word fotu on their T-shirts.

"What does fotu stand for?" they asked.

"Yes," said Peter. "I was wondering about that myself."

"That's easy," said Windshield Wiper. "Fotu stands for friend of the universe."

"Is that what you are?" asked one of the penguins.

"That's right," said Josh. "We are friends of the universe."

"What do you have to do to be a fotu?" asked another of the penguins.

"All you have to do," answered Josh, "is try to be good and honest and fair to all living things."

"I know someone like that," said a penguin.

"So do I," said another.

"Yes," said Windshield Wiper. "There are lots of friends of the universe everywhere."

"I'd like to be a fotu," said one of the younger penguins.

"Me too," said another.

As they walked on toward the north end of the island everyone talked and listened and laughed. But when they reached the top of a hill, Peter suddenly stopped.

"This is as far as I go," he said.

"You said you would show us the way," said Josh.

"And I did," said Peter. "This is the start of the north end of the island. You will find Blue just over the next hill."

"What are you afraid of?" asked Bamboo.

"I'm afraid of nothing," said Peter.

"Then why won't you come with us?" asked Bamboo.

"This is the way things have always been," said Peter.

Bamboo seemed to understand and they walked on without Peter. The north end of the island was just as crowded as the south and as a matter of fact, it was hard to tell where the south part ended and the north part began.

After a few more minutes of walking, they arrived at the water's edge. Captain was waiting for them.

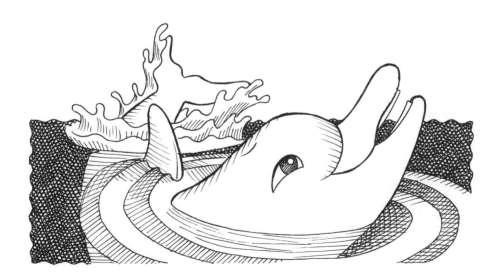

"I raced as fast as I could just to get here ahead of you," said Captain.

"Have you seen Blue?" asked Bamboo.

"She's still out playing with her friends," said Captain. "I'll tow you out to her."

"Let's go," said Windshield Wiper.

Everyone jumped into the water and Captain towed them out to where Blue was playing. Bamboo was not really sure of what he was going to say to Blue but that didn't bother him. There is a solution to every problem, thought Bamboo.

When they found Blue, Bamboo talked to her about all of the things Pilot had said. While all of this was taking place, Josh again noticed something which seemed very strange. This is impossible, thought Josh. And yet there it was.

Chapter 5

While Bamboo was talking with Blue, once again a group of fish had gathered about to listen in on what was going on. And there, sitting with all the others was the slow seahorse named Teacup.

Now there was nothing strange about the fish being curious and there was nothing wrong with them gathering about. But there was something very strange about Teacup being at the north end of the island. Josh went over and quietly talked with her.

"Teacup," said Josh. "When I met you, you told me you were a slow seahorse and that you sometimes have trouble keeping up with all the others."

"That's true," said Teacup.

"And when we first came up here to talk with Blue, you were here."

"That's true too," said Teacup.

17

"And when Captain towed us around to the south end of the island, once again there you were."

"I only wanted to be with everyone else," said the slow seahorse.

"And now Captain has just raced back up here and once again, you are here too."

"Here I am," agreed Teacup.

"But," said Josh, "a dolphin can swim very fast and although you swim so slow, you still made it here in the same time. How can that be?"

The slow seahorse smiled and said, "That was easy."

"It seems strange to me," said Josh.

"I'm here because I know a shortcut," said Teacup.

"A shortcut?" asked Josh.

"Yes," said Teacup. "I swim under the island."

"You can't swim under an island," laughed Josh.

"I can," said Teacup. "Come on. I'll show you."

While Bamboo talked with Blue, Josh followed Teacup toward the island and when they were close to the shoreline, Josh took a deep breath and followed Teacup down below the surface.

They were diving deeper and deeper when Teacup suddenly disappeared under a ledge. For a moment, Josh was worried about what had happened to the little seahorse. Where did she go, wondered Josh?

He dove under the ledge and there he found Teacup waiting for him. And under that same ledge he also learned why the slow seahorse could get from the north to the south end of the island so quickly. As they swam back to the surface, Josh thought about Teacup's shortcut and suddenly a lot of things started to make sense and then he knew why the penguins were having such problems. It's so simple, thought Josh. But was it also too late? There was no time to waste.

Josh and Teacup soon returned to where Bamboo was talking with Blue. They were still trying to figure out what to do.

"Bamboo," said Josh. "Thanks to Teacup, I think I know what the real problem is."

With this bit of news, everyone stopped talking.

"You're not going to believe this," said Josh, "but I just swam under this island."

"You can't swim under an island," said Windshield Wiper.

"Of course you can't," said Josh. "That's just it. This ice-covered island isn't an island. It's an iceberg."

"Are you sure?" asked Bamboo.

"Positive," said Josh. "And if both Blue and Pilot are telling the truth and their families are not getting much bigger, this can only mean one thing."

"I know I'm telling the truth," said Blue.

"Then why is it getting more and more crowded for the penguins?" asked Bamboo.

"Because they are living on an iceberg," said Josh. "And the iceberg is melting."

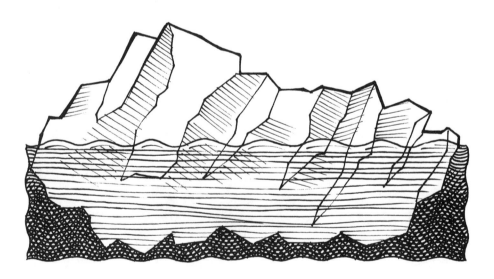

Chapter 6

The first thing everyone had to do was go and look for themselves. And sure enough, Josh was right.

"Our island really is an iceberg," said some of the penguins.

"And what if it is melting?" asked some of the others.

"I have noticed the water getting a bit warmer," said Captain.

Everyone talked at once. They were all worried about what would happen to them.

"What will we do?" asked Blue.

"We must stop this iceberg from melting," said Bamboo. "And the only way to do that is to push it back into colder water."

"That's impossible," laughed some of the penguins. "You can't push an iceberg."

"We can if we all push together," said Bamboo.

"Yes," said Josh. "If the north and the south penguins all get together and push, we just might be able to do it."

"The north penguins do not mingle with the south penguins," said Blue.

"That's crazy," said Windshield Wiper.

"There has to be another way," said Blue.

"It's your only hope," said Bamboo. "You must come with us and talk to Pilot."

"I will not go to the south end of the island," said Blue.

"You must," said Josh. "Your home is at risk. You must do something now."

Blue thought for a moment and then she said, "The only way I will talk to Pilot is if he comes here and talks with me."

"And what if he won't?" asked Josh.

"He better," said Windshield Wiper.

"We will have to go back down to the south end of the island and talk to him," said Bamboo.

"I'll take you," said Captain.

"Yes," said Josh. "And we can talk to all the penguins along the way and get them to help us."

"Let's go," said Windshield Wiper.

And off they went. Bamboo, Josh, Windshield Wiper and Mary all grabbed onto Captain's fin and once again they set off for the south end of the island.

Along the way they talked to lots of penguins. But every one of them said the same thing. They all said they would wait and see what Pilot and Blue decided was the best thing to do.

"Don't they want to save their home?" asked Mary.

Captain swam as fast as she could and they soon arrived at the south end of the island. They were told that Pilot was still playing with some of the other penguins and so they set out to find him.

Captain towed his friends along the shoreline and when they rounded a corner, in the distance they saw Pilot. But they were not the only ones who had seen the penguins playing.

"Look!" cried Josh. "A shark!"

Sure enough, much to everyone's horror, there was a shark attacking the penguins. And because Pilot was the closest, the shark was getting ready to grab him. And Pilot and his friends were so busy playing, they didn't even see the shark.

Captain could swim very fast and she raced ahead to save Pilot. But the shark could swim just as fast and it was much closer to the penguins. There was nothing Bamboo and the others could do but watch from a distance. When the shark was almost on top of Pilot, its mouth opened very wide and it got ready to chomp. Pilot still did not know that he was about to become a snack for the hungry shark. And Captain was too far away to help.

Chapter 7

Just as the hungry shark was about to grab Pilot, a black and white blur shot out from under the iceberg. It was much closer than Captain to where the penguins were playing and it raced ahead to warn Pilot. The shark's big mouth was stretched wide open and just as it was about to chew on Pilot, the black and white blur knocked Pilot out of the way.

The shark's attack was much too close for comfort and all of the penguins scattered off in different directions and hid along the shoreline. But the shark was still hungry and now it was mad too and so it went after the penguin who had saved Pilot's life. That penguin had not thought about it's own safety and because of this, it was in big trouble. The sleek shark could swim much faster and in no time was right on top of it. There was no time for the penguin to get to the shelter of the shoreline.

Once again the big shark's mouth opened wide. Just as the shark was about to chomp, Captain cut in and rammed the shark hard on its belly. This gave the penguin time to hide and after a short fight, the shark decided it didn't want to tangle with the angry dolphin and it went off to find something else to eat.

Pilot was very grateful for having his life saved and when he went over to say thank you, he was very surprised to learn that the penguin who had saved his life was none other than Blue.

"Why did you save me?" asked Pilot.

"I didn't know it was you," said Blue. "All I saw was a penguin in trouble and I wanted to help."

"Thank you for changing your mind about coming to the south end of the island," said Bamboo.

25

"It wasn't easy," said Blue, "but sometimes we have to do these things."

"Sometimes," said Bamboo.

"I don't understand," said Pilot.

"Like it or not," said Blue, "we are all a part of the same family and we need each other."

"What are you talking about?" asked Pilot.

"We've got some big problems," said Blue. "Our home is in trouble and the only way to save it is for all of us to work together."

Now Pilot was really confused. Blue and Bamboo went on to tell Pilot about their island being an iceberg and how it was melting. Pilot was no fool and after going to have a look for himself, he quickly agreed that the only to save their home was to try and push it back into colder water.

"Which way will we push it?" asked Josh.

"I know," said Captain. "I've travelled all over the place and the water to the north is much colder."

"So be it," said Bamboo. "We will push the iceberg to the north."

"Let's get all the penguins together!" said Pilot.

"The first time ever!" said Blue.

Pilot went off in one direction and Blue went off in another and they talked to all of the penguins and when they all heard about their island and how it melting, they all wanted to help.

Before long, all of the penguins had gathered at the south end of the island. Never before had so many penguins been together in one spot. There were penguins everywhere.

"I've never seen anything like it," said Josh.

"None of us have," said Pilot.

When all of the penguins were lined up along the shoreline and when everyone was ready to push, Bamboo counted, "One! Two! Three! And push!"

Everyone pushed. Even the little penguins pushed. They all tried their best.

But the iceberg did not move at all. Everyone groaned.

"We'll never move it," said one of the penguins."

"You can't move an iceberg," said another.

"What will we do?" asked a third penguin.

"There's always a way," said Bamboo.

"We just have to try harder," said Blue.

"Yes," said Pilot. "We can do it."

"Come on," said some of the others. "Let's try it again."

Everyone was excited and again they got ready to push.

Bamboo counted, "One! Two! Three! And push!"

Once again they all pushed. And this time they pushed harder than they had pushed before. This time they gave it their best shot.

"Push!" yelled Blue.

"Harder!" yelled Pilot.

Every one of those penguins pushed with everything they had. But the iceberg did not move.

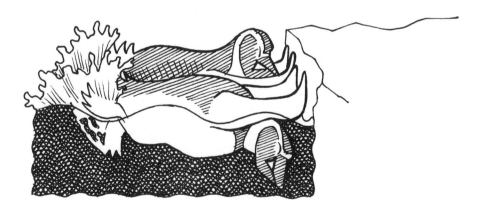

Chapter 8

"The island didn't move at all," said one of the penguins.

"Now what?" asked another.

"There must be something we can do," said Windshield Wiper.

While everyone tried to figure out what to do, a crowd of fish gathered around to see what the fuss was all about. This gave Mary an idea.

"Maybe we can get the fish to help push," said Mary.

"The fish?" asked a penguin.

"It's worth a try," said Pilot.

"What have we got to lose?"

asked Blue.

Pilot and Blue went over to the group of fish and asked if they would like to help.

"We'd love to help," said all of the fish.

"All the others can help too," said one.

"Let's go get them," said another.

Once again there was hope as everyone shot off in different directions to gather together all of the local sea creatures.

It took a while but everyone pitched in and soon the south end of the island was jammed. Big and small fish had come from all over to help. Even the lobsters and the crabs showed up. All of Captain's dolphin friends came too. Teddy Tuna dropped by to lend a fin. Even the starfish wanted to help. But the shark didn't come to help. And no one complained about that.

Finally, when everyone was ready, Blue started to line all of them up along the shoreline. The north and the south penguins lined up side by side with the dolphins and the fish and all the others. It was quite a sight.

"Is everyone ready?" asked Blue.

"We are ready," they all said.

"Then let's do it!" yelled Pilot.

Once again Bamboo counted, "One! Two! Three! And push!"

And then everyone pushed. The lobster's tails flashed and the penguin's flippers flipped. Everyone pushed as hard as they could. They all wanted to give it their best shot. They pushed and they pushed and they pushed. But try as they might, the iceberg did not move.

Some of the older penguins had pushed so hard, they almost passed out. Teddy Tuna was whacked. He was a bit of a lazy one

and in his whole life he had never worked so hard. But there wasn't one in the crowd who was willing to give it up.

"Let's try it again," they all said.

"We can do it!" they yelled.

Everyone cheered as once again they all lined up along the shoreline. When everyone was in place, again Bamboo counted, "One! Two! Three! And push!"

This time they pushed even harder than before. This time they were mad. This time that island was going to move. The water around the south end of the island was bubbling and swirling and frothing. No one in the entire crowd could push any harder. The starfish was pushing so hard, it started to spin like a top.

And then the island started to shake. It was starting to move. "Push harder!" yelled Pilot.

"It's moving!" cried Blue.

Everyone wanted to push harder and they tried their best to find some more strength. The island was shaking and some thought they could feel it starting to move.

"Push!" they yelled.

They were so close. But it just was not enough and the island stopped shaking. It still had not moved.

Chapter 9

"What bad luck," said a south penguin.

"Our island home turns out to be a melting iceberg," said a north penguin.

"Is it bad luck or good luck?" asked Bamboo.

All of the sea creatures tried to figure out what to do. As far as anyone knew, there were no other islands anywhere. The penguin's home was melting and they had nowhere to go.

"What will we do?" asked the penguins.

No one had an answer. Even the smart dolphins, who usually had an answer for everything, did not know what to do. Everyone who could help was there pushing. They had all given it their best shot but they could not move the iceberg.

"It's just too big," said Pilot.

"And we were so close," said Blue.

As they all lay floating in the water, Josh looked around at all of his new friends. They are a good bunch, thought Josh to himself. But when he looked around again and he realized that something was wrong.

"There's someone missing," said Josh.

Everyone looked around and they saw all their friends.

"We're all here," they said.

"No," said Josh. "Teacup is missing."

And sure enough, when everyone looked again, they all agreed.

"You're right," said Blue. "Where is she?"

They started to look around for the missing seahorse and within minutes she was found hiding under the iceberg.

"What are you doing under here?" asked Bamboo.

"I didn't want to get in the way," said Teacup.

"But we needed everyone to help push," said Pilot.

"And that includes you," said Blue.

"I didn't think I could make any difference," said the little seahorse.

"How do you know unless you try?" asked Bamboo.

"You might have made all the difference in the world," said Blue.

In her entire life, the slow seahorse had never been needed and this brought a smile to her face.

"Come on," said Pilot. "Let's give it another try."

They all raced back to the south end of the island. And to keep up with all the others, Teacup swam faster then she had ever gone before. They need me, thought Teacup to herself.

All the penguins, fish and dolphins lined up along the south shore of the iceberg. Bamboo, Windshield Wiper, Josh and Mary were there. So was Teddy Tuna, the starfish and all the others. And last but not least, right up there in the middle of them all was the slow seahorse named Teacup.

Everyone was ready. This time they were going to get that iceberg moving.

"This time we're going to do it," yelled Pilot.

"We can," said Bamboo, "if we believe we can."

"We believe!" yelled Blue.

Everyone cheered!

"Are we ready?" asked Bamboo.

Everyone cheered again! Teacup cheered too.

"All right then," yelled Bamboo. "Let's move this mountain of ice."

35

Another cheer rang out. They were ready.

Bamboo counted, "One! Two! Three! And push!"

You can imagine the sudden burst of energy when they all started to push. Every last muscle along that entire stretch of beach strained to the limit. Everyone gave it all they had. They wanted that island to move.

With all the kicking and pushing and shoving, once again the water started to swirl and bubble and froth. And as you might have guessed, once again the island started to shudder and shake.

"It's going to move!" yelled Pilot.

"Push harder!" yelled Blue.

They were all pushing as hard as they could. No one could push any harder. The island was shaking like never before. It was so close to moving.

"We can do it!" yelled Pilot.

It was then that Teacup closed her eyes and from deep inside she called for strength and with her little fin she pushed. And in that same moment, the iceberg started to move.

"It's moving!" yelled Josh.

Everyone could feel it. The iceberg was starting to move. Slowly at first, but it started to move. Everyone cheered! They were doing it. They were moving the iceberg.

Just as the iceberg was starting to move, Teacup heard something.

"What is that?" she asked

Mary and Josh heard it too. Soon all the others could hear it. One by one they all heard strange sounds coming from somewhere far away.

"Where is that coming from?" asked some of the penguins.

Everyone stopped pushing and they all listened.

"What is it?" they asked.

36

Chapter 10

"I've never heard anything like it," said Pilot.

As everyone listened, the strange sounds were slowly getting louder.

"Sounds like it's coming this way," said Blue.

"Let's go and see what it is," said Peter the penguin.

"What about our iceberg?" asked Blue.

"We'll come right back," said Pilot.

"Grab onto my fin," said Captain to Bamboo and the others. "I'll tow you."

And off they went. The entire group swam off to see where the strange sounds were coming from. Teacup went along and she soon found that if she worked very hard, she could in fact keep up with all the others. This pleased her very much.

As they swam on, the sounds were getting louder and louder.

A few of the older penguins started to remember hearing these same sounds when they were very young but that was a long time ago and for longer than most could remember, the seas had been silent.

When they were very close to the source of the sounds, everyone stopped swimming. They all sat still and listened. Some of the younger penguins started to get nervous. So did Mary.

"Don't be afraid," said one of the older penguins.

In the beginning they could see only the sun's light shining down through the deep blue sea. Moments later, something emerged from the shadows. It was huge and grey and at first only the front part could be seen. But as it slowly moved into the light, more and more of its giant body was revealed and soon everyone could see that this sea creature was bigger than anything anyone had ever seen.

"It's a whale," said Josh.

As the whale swam closer, everyone sat still and admired its slow and graceful movement. When it passed, the whale looked at the entire crowd. It was big enough to gobble up at least fifty of the penguins, and yet no one was afraid. In that whale's steady gaze everyone saw and felt a gentle love which was very soothing.

After the first whale passed, the music of the sea grew louder as more and more of the whales started to appear from out of the

shadows. Soon the entire area was filled with the sights and the sounds of the huge whales singing their gentle song. There were even baby whales following along behind their mothers.

"They sound like angels singing," said Peter the penguin.

Everyone sat quietly in the water and they all listened to the whale's beautiful music.

Chapter 11

When the whales had finished singing their song, they came over to meet everyone.

"Hello," said the leader of the whales. "My name is Kiki."

After they had all introduced themselves, there were lots of questions for the whales.

"Where do you come from?" asked Pilot.

"We have always been nearby," said Kiki.

"I have never seen you," said Blue.

"And I have never heard your music," said Pilot.

"That's because we have been waiting," said Kiki.

"Waiting for what?" asked Blue.

"For a long time we have watched the north and the south penguins argue. And now, because your home is melting, we have watched you learn to trust each other. This pleases us very much."

"Is that why you are singing?" asked Pilot.

"We sing because we are happy," said Kiki.

"I'm happy too," said Teacup. "Can I sing along with you."

"Anyone can," said Kiki.

"We never knew you were watching us," said Pilot.

"What is done is done," said Kiki. "Now is the time for all of us to work together."

"You're going to help us push our island back into colder water?" asked Blue.

"Of course," said Kiki. "With us helping, it won't take long at all."

"Let's go move it," said Pilot.

"I can help too," said Teacup.

As everyone swam back to the south end of the island, they sang along with the whales. When they got there, the whales lined up along the shoreline. For the huge whales, pushing the iceberg would be easy. The penguins and the dolphins still wanted to help and they lined up beside the whales. The lobsters and the crabs thought they would like to get in on the fun and they lined up too. So did the starfish. Lazy old Teddy Tuna decided to sit this one out because he had strained a fin on the last push. Bamboo, Josh, Windshield Wiper and Mary lined up with all the others.

"It's not often you get to work with a bunch like this," said Josh.

This time Teacup did not hide. The slow seahorse was no bigger than one of the whale's eyelashes but still she lined up beside everyone else.

"I can make a difference," said Teacup.

"Are we ready?" asked Bamboo.

Everyone cheered!

"Here we go again," said Bamboo. He counted, "One! Two! Three! And push!"

This time the island didn't stand a chance. Without even a shudder or a shake, the island just started to move. The whales were so big and strong, they set that iceberg in motion right away.

Teacup was right there in the middle of them all, pushing with all of her strength. It is hard to say just how much of a difference she made in terms of pushing power, but her efforts did inspire the others to give it their best and that helped a lot.

All that afternoon, they kept moving the iceberg into colder and colder water. Every once in a while some of them needed a rest. But the whales never did. They just kept on pushing. When the water got very cold, Pilot called for everyone to stop.

45

"This is far enough," said Pilot.

"We did it," they yelled.

"We saved our home," they all yelled.

"With a little help from our friends," said Blue.

Everyone cheered. They were all very happy. They had set out to do something and by working together, they had done it.

"Let's have a party," said one of the penguins.

"Great idea," said the others.

And what a party it was. All of the friends who helped push the iceberg started to swim about. The dolphins leapt in the air and the penguins splashed all around.

Chapter 12

"This is a great party," said Josh.

All the dolphins were swimming circles around everyone. The penguins zipped back and forth with the fish and of course the whales sang their songs.

Late in the day Bamboo called out to Josh, Mary and Windshield Wiper.

"It's time for us to get going," said Bamboo.

"Already?" asked Josh.

"We promised your mom we would be home in time for dinner," said Bamboo.

Although no one wanted to leave, Bamboo was right. They had made a promise and now they must be on their way.

Those that could got out of the water. All the others floated along the shoreline.

"Thank you," said Pilot.

"I'm glad we could help," said Bamboo.

"I hope your home will be okay," said Josh.

"We will work together and take better care of it," said Blue.

"And we will help them," said Kiki.

"Will you keep singing your songs?" asked Mary.

"I think we will be singing for a long, long time," said Kiki. Bamboo's ship was parked nearby. He climbed aboard and passed out an armload of white T-shirts.

"Hey everyone," said Windshield Wiper. "We have gifts for all of you."

Josh and Mary handed out a T-shirt to everyone who had helped push the iceberg. The penguins put theirs on right away. Printed on the front of each shirt was the word fotu.

"I'm a fotu!" said a penguin.

"I'm a friend of the universe," said another.

The dolphins and the crabs and the lobsters got a shirt too. So did

Teacup and the starfish. When the dolphins put theirs on, they looked kind of silly. But the dolphins didn't care. They thought the shirts looked great. Teacup's was way too big but she didn't care either. The starfish tried to put hers on but she could not because she has five arms.

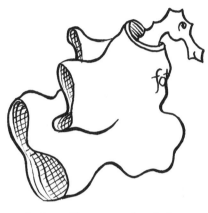

"Oh well," said the starfish, "I'll figure something out."

"I'm sorry," said Bamboo to the whales, "but we don't have any shirts big enough to fit you."

"That's okay," said Kiki. "It's enough for us to know we are like everyone else."

"As a matter of fact," said Blue, "things might be better for all of us if we were more like you."

"What do you mean?" asked Kiki.

"I think that you know a lot more than you let on," said Blue.

"Perhaps," said Kiki.

"Will you teach us?" asked Pilot.

"There is much to learn," said Kiki.

"We have lots of time," said Blue.

"Then let us begin by singing a song together," said Kiki.

And that is the way Bamboo, Josh, Windshield Wiper and

Mary left the island. After everyone said their goodbyes, the visitors to Paradise climbed into their ship and gently lifted off the ice.

As they closed the door, the last thing they heard was the sound of the whales singing with the penguins and the dolphins and the fish. The beautiful music could be heard for miles and there were many distant sea creatures who were listening. Some of the older ones remembered hearing this same kind of music when they were very young and it pleased them to once again be hearing these songs of joy and trust and love.

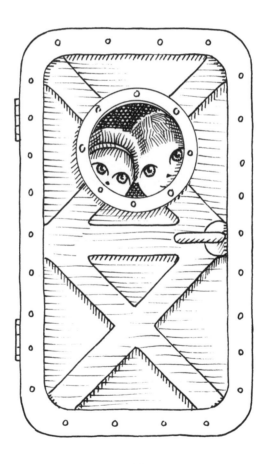

A note from the author

In October each year I travel to Peninsula Valdes, which is in the southern part of Argentina more commonly known as Patagonia. The reason for my annual trek to this remote coastal area is because of my participation in an aerial photographic survey of the southern right whale population which gathers each year to mate and to give birth to their calves. My participation in this study allows me to experience some of the very best nature has to offer.

Three hundred kilometers south of Peninsula Valdes is Punta Tombo, the land-based home of over one million Magellanic penguins which return every September to lay their eggs and forty days later, to watch over the hatching of their chicks.

Prior to the publication of this book, while in Patagonia I journeyed to Punta Tombo and spent four incredible days with the penguins. The pictures on the following pages were taken at Punta Tombo.

J.C.A.

Welcome to Paradise.

This male and female are grooming each other.

Building a comfortable nest is important work.

Look at the size of their feet!

As far as the eye can see, penguins.

Keeping an egg warm for forty days.

A two-way road for penguins going to and
from the sea for food and a drink of water.

Washing is important too.

Penguins sometimes mate for life.

Who is watching who?

Photo by: Dieter Engel

This book we are all so proud to be a part of would not be in your hands today if not for the creative input and artistic skills of Michael Engel. He sits in his studio, surrounded by his art and his Macintosh computer and he creates wonderful things.